The BIG Red Book of Beginner Books

D0090548

The BIG Red Book of Beginner Books

by
P. D. Eastman,
Joan Heilbroner and P. D. Eastman,
Robert Lopshire,
Mike McClintock and Fritz Siebel,
Al Perkins and Eric Gurney,
Marilyn Sadler and Roger Bollen

Random House New York

Contents

I Want to Be Somebody New!

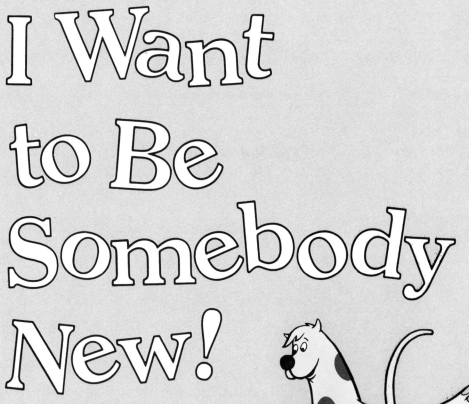

by
Robert Lopshire

For Selma, with love

Once I wanted
to be in the zoo.
And that was the day
I first met you.

You said that the zoo
was not for me.

The circus, you said,

was where I should be.

And so the circus
is where I went.
I did my tricks
with spots on a tent.
I put my spots
way up in the air.
I put my spots
just everywhere!

My tricks with spots
were lots of fun.
But no more spot tricks!
I am done!

Now I want to be
somebody new.
So here's a new trick
I'll show to you!

Ready! Get set now.
One, two, three...

15

Now look and tell me
what you see.

An elephant
is what we see!
Why, you are as big
as big can be!

But being that big
cannot be fun.
Say! You must weigh
at least a ton!

You cannot walk

up on this fence...

or squeeze between
these circus tents.

The door of your house
is now too small.
You can't get through
that door at all!

You can't go here.

You can't go there.

You can't go

much of anywhere!

24

You cannot sit
in your old chair.
Your new rear end
won't fit in there.
You're very big.
You're very fat.
We do not care
for you like that.

25

Every word of what you say is true.

Okay. So I'll be someone new.

Ready? Get set now. One, two, three...

Now look
and tell me
what you see.

A tall giraffe
is what we see.
You are as tall
as tall can be!

But being that tall can't be any fun.

You're taller now than everyone!

Your head is now so high in the air,

it's hard to see your face up there.

And we can see

from way down here

a bird is flying in your ear!

We do not like

to see you tall.

We do not like you

tall at all!

Every word of what
you say is true.
Okay. So I'll be
someone new.
Ready? Get set now.
One, two, three...
Now look and tell me
what you see!

A mouse! A mouse!

That's what we see.

You are as small

as small can be.

34

Well, what do you think?
I'm asking you.
Do I look good
this way to you?

We did not like you
fat or tall.
And now you're
very much too small.
Your chair is now
too big for you.

And now your door
is too big, too!
You cannot
open up your door.
And that's not all.
There's much, much more!

A mouse cannot
go out and play.
A mouse must hide
inside all day.

And a mouse must never

make a sound.

Because that's what brings

the cats around.

There are traps put out
to catch a mouse
because no one wants one
in their house.

We did not like you
fat or tall,
and now you know
what's wrong with small!

Okay! Okay!
Okay, you two.
I'll make myself
be someone new.
Ready? Get set now.
One, two, three…
Now look and tell me
what you see!

Oh, no you don't!
You stop right there!
We like you
and we really care.

We liked you best,
a whole, whole lot,
when you were just
our old friend Spot.
So do your trick
with your one, two, three...
But show us what we want to see!

Say! You are right!
As right can be!
And it does feel best
to be just me!

Sam and the Firefly

Written and Illustrated by

P. D. EASTMAN

For Mary,
Tony, and Alan

The moon was up
when Sam came out.

"Now is the time for fun," he said.
"who," said Sam, "who!
Who wants to play?"
But no one said a thing.

Then Sam looked about.
The fox was asleep
and the jay was asleep.
The dog was asleep
and the hog was asleep.
The sheep was asleep,
and so was the cow.

Then Sam went down to the lake.

But no one was there.

All he could see was the moon
and the shine of the moon
on the water.

"It takes two to have fun.
WHO," said Sam, "WHO!

Who wants to play?"

But no one said a thing.

Then Sam saw a light!

He saw the light hop.

He saw the light jump.

It went here, it went there.

It went on, it went off.

But no one said a thing.

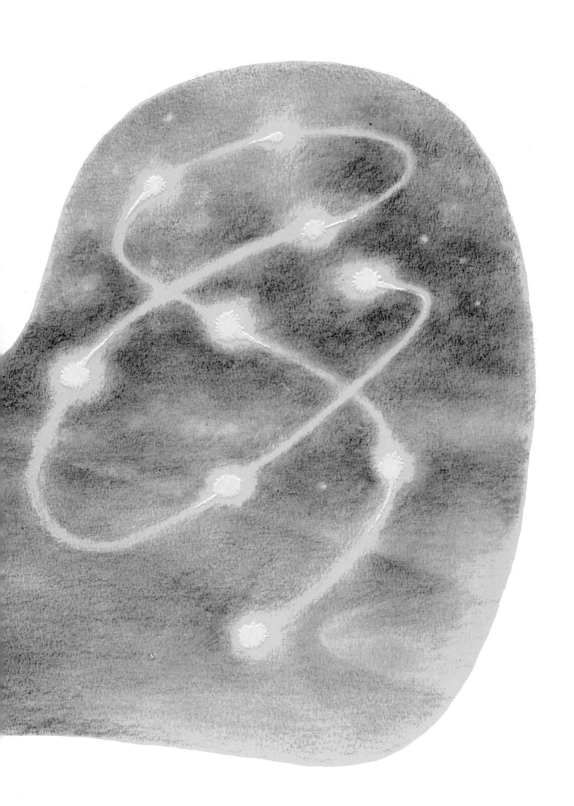

56

Then the light hit Sam
on the top of his head!
The light said, "BOO!"
"Who made that BOO?" asked Sam.
"Who are you?"

"I am a firefly.

My name is GUS.

And I have a trick I can do

with my light. Look, look!

I can put it on

and KEEP it on,

like this."

Then Sam saw something new!

The firefly made lines
with his light.

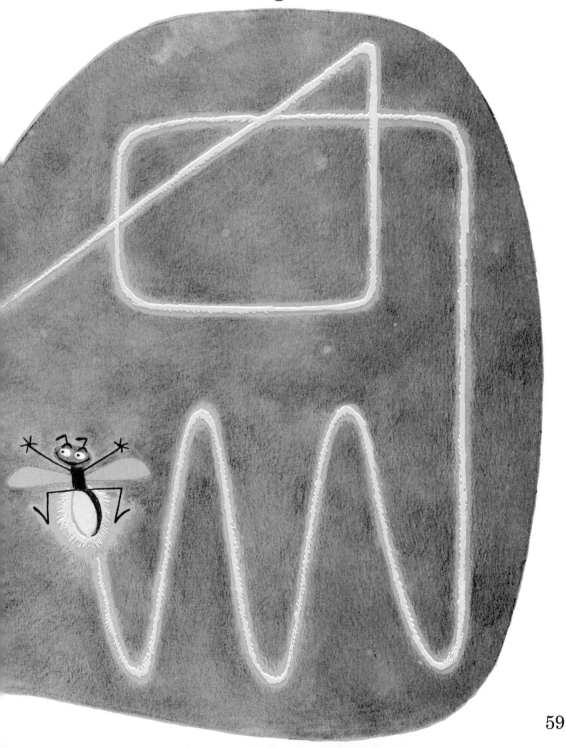

60

"Say!" said Sam.

"WHAT a trick! This is NEW!

Oh, the things we can do
with a trick like THAT!

Let me show you.

Now put on your light
and KEEP it on.

Then you do what I do,"
he said to Gus.

Then Sam went up,
and Gus went after him.
When Sam went down,
down went the firefly too.
Where Sam went,
Gus went.

Then Sam stopped,
and Gus stopped too.

"Now just look there," said Sam.

"See what we did!"

GUS AND SAM

"Why! We made WORDS,
BIG words!" said Gus the Firefly.
"Say, I LIKE this game!
I want to do it again.
This word trick is fun.
Come on. Make MORE words."

So away the two went,

Gus after Sam.

They made lots of new words.

They made FISH.

They made WISH.

They made HOUSE

and A MOUSE.

Then

FOX

DOG

CAT

YES

NO

KANGAROO

and THERMOMETER!

FISH WISH

HOUSE   A MOUSE

FOX

DOG CAT

YES NO

KANGAROO

THERMOMETER

Sam and Gus made a lot
more words.

THEN . . .

Sam looked about.

He was all alone!

WHERE was Gus?

Then Sam looked down.

He saw some cars.

And there was the firefly
down by the cars!

"Come back here!" called Sam.

"What are you up to?"

What was Gus up to?

Gus made some words.

Gus made GO FAST and SLOW.

He made GO RIGHT
and GO LEFT.

And DID those cars GO!

They went BASH!

They went SMASH!

Gus did words
that made the cars CRASH.

Oh, what a mess those cars were in!

"Dear me!" said Sam.

"This will not do!

He should not do THIS!

Gus did a bad trick
with those words."

"Now see here, Gus . . ."

But Gus would NOT see.

He would not hear.

"YOW wow!

I like to make words,

LOTS of words," he said.

"I LIKE this game!

Let me be, you old GOOSE, you!"

And away he went.

"Stop, Gus! Stop!
Come back!" called Sam.
"That was a BAD trick.
Come back here now.
Bad tricks are not fun!"

"Oh, go on home!" said the firefly.
"You old GOOSE! You old HEN!
What do YOU know about fun?
GOOD-BY!" And away Gus went.

Now Gus did more tricks.

He did word tricks
on some airplanes.

He made them go up.

He made them go down.

He made them go this way.

He made them go that way.

NOW what a mess
the airplanes were in!

"No, Gus! No!" said Sam.

But Gus did not want to stop.

Not yet. This was fun!

Then Sam saw Gus
do another bad trick.

It made the firefly laugh
and laugh.

It was funny
to see them go in free
to the movie show!

"Stop your tricks," called Sam.

"No more words!

Stop, Gus! Stop!

Now STOP!"

But Gus the Firefly did NOT stop.

"I have one more trick," he said.

"A LITTLE trick.

Look, Sam! Look!

A ONE WORD trick!"

Then Gus did his little trick,
his ONE WORD trick.

He did a BAD trick

He did it to the Hot Dog Man.

He made the word COLD
near the top of the stand.

The men looked up.

They saw what Gus did.

"We want our Hot Dogs HOT,
not COLD!

Good-by," they said.

Gus did not see the Hot Dog Man,
the man with the net and the jar.

"Look out!" called Sam.

"Look out, Gus!
The Hot Dog Man is MAD!"

"I will GET that firefly,"
said the Hot Dog Man.

"I will take him away from here.
He will not play another
trick on ME!"

Then something hit Gus!

He was in a net!

THEN . . .

GUS THE FIREFLY WAS IN A JAR!

"Let me OUT!"

Gus hit at the walls of the jar!

He hopped about!

He jumped up and down!

But it did no good.

There was no way to get out.

Then Gus in the jar
was in a car!
The car went away fast.
Where would it take him?
Would he do more tricks?
Would he make more words?
Would he have fun again with his light?
Would Gus get out of the jar?

Gus did not know it,
but Sam was there too.
He was near by
in back of the car.
"Oh, what can I do?" said Sam.
"I have to get Gus out of that jar.
But how? How CAN I get him out?"
Sam was sad.

And Gus was sad too.

"I should have stopped
when Sam said NO.

I was bad.

I just had to have fun," said Gus.

"I wish Sam were here
to get me out."

The car went on.

Then it stopped with a BUMP!

It stopped on some tracks.

The car would not go!

The Hot Dog Man got out.

Then he looked down the tracks.

What did he see?

He saw a TRAIN!

Sam saw it too!
What would he do?
There was just ONE way
to stop that train!

Sam went to the car.

He took the jar,

the jar with Gus!

THEN . . .

He let the jar fall.

CRASH! And Gus was out!

"You can save the car, Gus!

You can stop the train!

You know what to do!

DO IT!" said Sam.

And the firefly did it!

He made the word STOP.

He did it fast and he did it BIG.

He did it a lot.

He made lots of big STOPS.

"YOW wow, Gus!" called Sam.

"At LAST you did a GOOD trick!"

"Look!
It says STOP!
Look down there!
A car on the track!
STOP THE TRAIN!"

The train DID stop!

And just in time.

"What a trick!" they all said.

"A good, GOOD trick!

HOORAY for the firefly!

He stopped the train!"

But Sam and Gus did not hear.

They had gone away.

Sam looked at Gus
as the sun came up.

"Now the morning light is here,
and no one can see your tricks!

It is time we went home to bed,"
said Sam.

So Sam went back
to his home in the tree,
and Gus went back to the lake.

But night after night,
when the moon comes up,
Gus the Firefly
comes back to play.

STOP THAT BALL!

BY MIKE McCLINTOCK

ILLUSTRATED BY FRITZ SIEBEL

I hit my ball. I made it fly.

I hit my ball as it went by.

It went around and then came back.

I gave my ball another WHACK!

I hit it high.

I hit it low.

I hit so hard the string let go!

The string let go.

There went my ball.

Away up high,

Out past the wall!

So I ran fast around the wall.

I had to get my big red ball.

I saw it jump. I saw it roll,

And head right for an open hole.

The hole was deep. The hole was black.

How could I get my red ball back?

What could I do?

Say! This was bad!

This was the only ball I had.

And then a man put out his head.

"You hit me with your ball!" he said.

He was so mad he sent my ball

Way down the hill. I saw it fall.

I saw my red ball take a hop

And you know where I saw it stop!

I saw it hop right on a truck.

Oh, what a shame! Oh, what bad luck!

The truck went down the hill, and so,

I ran as fast as I could go.

"Look here!" I called.

I called out, "Say!

You must not take my ball away."

At last the truck came to a stop,

And my red ball was up on top.

I saw the truck back up to dump.

The sand came out.

I had to jump!

The sand came out.

So did my ball.

I saw it jump and bump a wall.

I saw it jump right in a box.

I saw it land up on some blocks.

And there it sat.
I said, "I bet
That ball will not
Be hard to get."

Oh! Oh! Now here was something new!

The box went up!

My ball went, too!

It went up high.

What should I do?

I just could not sit here and whine.

I had to get that ball of mine.

"Here is your ball," called out a man.

"Now run and get it if you can!"

And then he gave my ball a kick.

Oh what a trick! Oh what a trick!

Now, could I get it? I could try!

My dog ran fast and so did I.

But not a thing went right that day.

That dog of mine got in my way.

Then down I went, and so did he.

My ball went on ahead of me.

My big red ball went on its way.

Would things go on like this all day?

A man said, "Stop!

Stop! Keep away!

Do not go near that hill, I say!

We are about to blow it up,

So stop right here,

And hold your pup!"

There was my ball—my only ball.

I could not get it after all!

Then BOOM! BOOM! BOOM!

Oh, what a thump!

I saw the hill just kind of jump.

And then it shot up in the air,

And bits of it went here and there.

Where was my ball?

Where did it go?

I could not see it high or low.

Then, there it was! High as a kite!
Now I could get my ball all right.
I said, "I know it must come down.
And it will fall somewhere in town.
Then I can find it. Yes, I can!"
And so I ran and ran and ran.

I saw a house on fire ahead.

"My ball must not land there!" I said.

"For if it does, it's gone for ever!

And I will never get it! Never!"

But then some water

Shot up high.

It hit my ball

And made it fly.

Boy! Was I happy!

This was fine!

Now I could get

That ball of mine!

It got away from me somehow.

My ball was in a ball game now.

It hit the man who sold the pop!

It went right on! It would not stop.

It went right for the man at bat.

I called, "Oh! no, do not hit that!"

Then, WHACK!

He hit a long home run

With my red ball!

My only one!

Here came my ball!

It hit a tree!

And POW!

It just about hit me!

Then on it went.

How could this be?

Could this go on all day and night?

It could, you know, and it just might.

This might go on all night and day!

I saw it go another way!

Now who could say where it might land!

I saw it head right for a band!

I saw a fat man in the band.

He had a fat horn in his hand.

Oh, what a thing to get into!

If it went there,

What could I do?

Oh, what bad luck!
My ball was stuck!

And so the fat man could not play,
For my red ball was in the way.
I saw him blow with all his might.
Oh, could he blow it out all right?

Oh, what a blow!
My ball shot out!
And it was gone,
Or just about.

I saw my ball head for a gun.

And then—oh, boy!—how I did run!

My ball came down, just like a shot.

What did it do?

Why, you know what!

I got up on that gun so fast!

Now I might get my ball at last!

I put my head down in to see,

But then a man took hold of me.

He took me down.

"Get back!" he said.

"That gun

Could blow away your head!"

Then BOOM!

BOOM! BOOM!

Oh, what a thump!

I saw the gun

Just kind of jump.

It shot my ball

Up in the air.

How high would it go now?

And where?

My ball went high up past the band,

The tree, the game, the fire, the sand,

The box, the blocks, then past the man

Down in the hole.

I ran and ran!

My ball went over all the town!

And do you know where it came down?

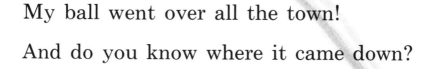

My ball was home!

I ran so fast!

Now I could have my ball at last!

And I could put it on the string!

I was so happy I could sing!

But by the time I got home, too,

Someone—

I do not know just who—

Had put my ball back on the string.

That was a kind of funny thing!

But I was happy anyway.

I had my ball

And I could play!

I hit my ball. I made it fly.

I hit my ball as it came by.

It went around and then came back.

I gave my ball another WHACK!

I hit it high.

I hit it low.

I saw the string let go,

And then

My ball was on its way again!

Could this go on all day and night?

It could, you know, and it just might!

Robert the
Rose Horse

by Joan Heilbroner

Illustrated by P. D. Eastman

To Peter and Barbara, with love
and
To Troop B of New York's Mounted Police

Robert was a happy little horse.

He lived on a farm.

He lived with his mother
and father.

One day Robert had a party.

It was his birthday.

All his farm friends came

to the party.

They had a big cake.

"Happy birthday, Robert,"

said all of his friends.

"Happy birthday to you."

The cake was very pretty.

It had big red roses all around it.

Robert liked those red roses.

He put his nose right into one.

He took a big sniff.

Then Robert got a funny feeling.

His eyes began to itch.

His nose began to itch.

And then . . .

"KERCHOO!" Robert sneezed.

What a sneeze!

Up went his farm friends.

Up went the cake.

Up went the roses.

And Robert fell down flat.

His mother called the doctor.

The doctor looked at Robert.

"Say AH," said the doctor.

"AH," said Robert.

"AHA!" said the doctor.

"I know what made him sneeze."

"I know I am right," said the doctor.

"You will see.

Here, Robert.

Take a little sniff."

Robert put his nose

into those roses.

He took a little sniff.

Again his nose began to itch.

Again his eyes began to itch.

KER

"KERCHOO!" went Robert.

BANG went the window.

BANG went the door.

Up went the roses.

And the doctor fell down flat.

"I was right," said the doctor.

"Roses are very bad for you.

There are too many roses

on this farm.

You must get away from them.

You must go to the city."

So Robert had to go.

"Good-by," he said

to his mother and father.

"I will be all right in the city.

I will find work. I will find a job."

Robert did find a job in the city.

He went to work for a milk man.

He took the milk man and his wagon

all around the city.

It was a good job.

And Robert was happy.

Robert liked this kind of job.

Then one day a man walked
right next to Robert.
The man had a flower in his coat.
The flower in his coat was a rose.

A rose!

And right under his nose!

Robert got that funny feeling again.

His nose began to itch.

And his eyes began to itch.

And . . .

"KERCHOO!" went Robert.

CRASH went the wagon.

SPLASH went the milk.

Up went the milk man.

And the man with the rose

fell down flat.

"Go away!" the milk man told Robert.

"You can not work for me any more."

So Robert began to look for work again.

But it was hard for a horse

to find a job.

He looked for many days.

HORSE
WANTED

One day he saw some horses.

They had people on them.

"Say! I could do work like that,"
said Robert.

"I will ask for a job."

Robert went to the door.

A man came out.

"You look like a good horse,"

the man told Robert.

"You can work for me.

But you will have to work hard.

You will have to do

everything you are told."

So Robert went to work.

He did just as he was told.

When he was told to go slow,

he went slow.

When he was told to go fast,

he went fast.

Robert did everything he was told.

"I like this work," Robert said.

"And I am going to keep this job."

Then one day

he took a woman for a ride.

Everything was going well.

But all at once . . .

"Look!" the woman said.

"Look at those pretty roses.

I want those roses.

Robert, take me over there at once."

What could Robert do?

He had to do as he was told.

He took the woman

to the roses.

Again, he got that
funny feeling.
His nose began to itch.
His eyes began to itch.

And . . .

"KERCHOO!" went Robert.

Away went the wagon.

Away went the flowers.

Up went the woman.

And the flower man

fell down flat.

KERCHOO

Once more Robert

was out of a job.

Robert had to look for work again.

He looked and looked.

Fathers had work.

Mothers had work.

Every one had some kind of work.

But there were not many
jobs for a horse.

Robert walked and walked.

He looked and looked.

Then at last

Robert saw something.

He saw a job he could do!

He could be

a police horse!

"I will go in.

I will ask for the job,"

he said.

When Robert came out

he was a police horse.

He was a good police horse.

He did all kinds of police work.

One day Robert worked on Bank Street.

Some men came down the street.

Three men!

One of them had a black bag.

They went into the bank.

Robert did not see them.

Then all at once . . .

Some one called out:

"Help! Police! Help!"

Robert looked around.

He saw the three men.

They were robbers!

Bank robbers!

The robbers ran right at Robert.

They ran right over him.

And away they went.

Robert got up fast!

He had to stop those robbers!

But how?

How could he do it?

And then . . .

Robert saw a rose!

It was not a big rose.

But it was a rose!

Robert began to think.

He began to think fast.

Robert went over to that rose.

He put his nose

right in that rose!

He took a sniff.

A big, big sniff!

And he began to get that

old funny feeling.

His eyes began to itch.

His nose began to itch.

THEN . . .

231

KER

Robert sneezed.

Never was there a sneeze

like it!

Away went cats.

Away went hats.

Up went dogs.

Down came birds.

BANG went the guns.

Up went the black bag.

And the robbers fell

down flat.

"Hooray! Hooray for Robert!"

every one yelled.

The bank man was happy.

The policemen were happy.

Every one was happy.

Robert had stopped the robbers!

He had sneezed the robbers flat!

The next day there was a party.

It was for Robert.

His mother and father came.

His farm friends came.

The doctor came.

All the policemen came, too.

Then one of them got up.

"Robert," he said, "I have

something for you."

237

"ROSES!" yelled the doctor.

"Hold on to your hats.

Here comes a sneeze!

Robert will sneeze us all to Chicago!"

Robert took a little sniff.

His nose did NOT itch.

His eyes did NOT itch.

Then Robert took a big, big sniff.

He did NOT get that funny feeling.

That big Kerchoo had done it.

Robert at last was all sneezed out.

And roses never made Robert sneeze again.

The Digging-est Dog

BY AL PERKINS ILLUSTRATED BY ERIC GURNEY

For
Dennis, Douglass, and Derek
with love

I was the saddest dog you could ever see,
Sad because no one wanted me.
The pet shop window was my jail.
The sign behind me said, "For Sale."

I was tied to a bare, hard floor of stone.

I could not even dig for a bone.

I was living all of my life alone,

A dog that no one wanted to own.

244

And then one day, at half-past four,
Sammy Brown came in the door.
Sam took one look at me and cried,
"Why are you tied up here inside?

"I've always wanted a dog like you,
So I'll tell you what I'm going to do.
I'll take you out to the farm with me.
You'll play outdoors where you should be."

I felt as happy as a pup
When Sam paid the man and picked me up.
He rubbed my ears. He scratched my head.
"I think I'll call you Duke," he said.

Sam gave me a collar. He gave me a lead.

We left that shop at tre-men-dous speed.

We went a long way out of town.

We came to the farm of Sammy Brown.

It was the nicest place I'd ever seen,

A pretty white house in a field of green.

And in the shade of the apple tree,
A special dog house just for me!

Next morning, while Sam did his chores,

He let me run and play outdoors.

I'd never played outdoors before.

I'd always lived on that hard floor.

I'd never run on nice soft ground.

Now I barked with joy as I ran around.

Sam looked at me and scratched his head.
"Duke, you need some friends," he said.

He blew his whistle. He blew a blast.

And many dogs came running fast.

I'd never met a dog before.

Now I was meeting six or more.

They walked around and looked at me.

They looked me over carefully.

Then, at last, I heard them say,

"He's one of us. He'll be okay."

One dog, who wasn't very big,

Suddenly began to dig.

The others started digging too.

But that was something I could not do.

I'd never learned to dig in that store.

How could I, on that hard stone floor?

I tried to dig, but, alas, I couldn't.

I wiggled my paws. My paws just wouldn't.

I fell on my ear. I fell on my face.

I fell on myself all over the place.

The others said, "Duke may be big,
But he's no good! He cannot dig."
They stuck their noses in the air.
They walked away. They left me there.

"I'll teach you, Duke," cried Sammy Brown.
"I'll show you how to dig deep down."
He crouched beside me. With his hand
He dug a hole in a pile of sand.

I tried it too. But still I couldn't.
I wiggled my paws. My paws just wouldn't.
I'd never learned to dig in that store.
How could I, on that hard stone floor?

Sammy sighed.

I almost cried.

My eyes and nose were full of dirt.

My paws and claws and elbows hurt.

I had a pain across my back.

I knew I'd never get the knack.

Sam felt sad, and I felt bad.

If only I could make him glad!

We both knew I'd never get it right.

Sam and I couldn't sleep that night.

So, when the sun rose in the sky,

I thought I'd give it one more try.

I wiggled one paw. I saw it could.

I wiggled the other. I saw it would.

I could dig with my paws.
I could dig with my claws.
I felt no pain across my back.
I knew at last I had the knack!

Sammy Brown looked out at me.

He saw me digging happily.

"Good for you, Duke!" Sammy cried.

"I knew you'd do it if you tried."

So I dug farther. I dug faster.

I dug and dug to please my master.

I dug up grass. I dug up weeds.
I dug up daisies. I dug up seeds.

274

I dug up the fence. I dug up the gates.
I dug up the garden of Mrs. Thwaites.

I dug up the rooster. I dug up the hens.
I dug up the sheep and pigs in their pens.

I dug and dug. I couldn't stop.
I dug up the barber in his shop.

I dug up Mister Rodney Thayer,
Sitting in the barber's chair.

I dug my way right through the town.
I dug a lot of buildings down.

I was having so much fun!
I dug up Highway Eighty-One.

I came to a hill. I dug to the top.
But all of a sudden I had to stop.

Right in front of me, looking down,
There stood my master, Sammy Brown!

Sam didn't smile or pat my head.
He only glared at me and said,
"I'm sending you back to that animal store.
They'll tie you to that hard stone floor,
And you'll never, *never* dig any more."

I couldn't run. I couldn't hide.

Dogs came at me from every side.

And then suddenly I knew

There was just one thing for me to do.

I ran away from Sammy Brown.

I dug a hole that went straight down.

I left him standing up on top.

I dug and dug. I didn't stop.

How deep I dug I could not tell.

But soon I found I'd dug a well!

Mud and water up to my chin!

What a fix I now was in!

I started to sink. I started to yelp.

"Help!" I yelped.

"Help! Help! Help! Help!"

I could hear them way above my head.
I could hear every word they said.
One dog growled, "He wrecked our town.
This serves him right. Just let him drown."

But Sam cried, "Duke! You've been bad.
You've made me sad instead of glad.
But we're not going to let you die.
We'll get you out. At least, we'll try!"

Then at last I heard him shout,
"Maybe we can pull you out!"

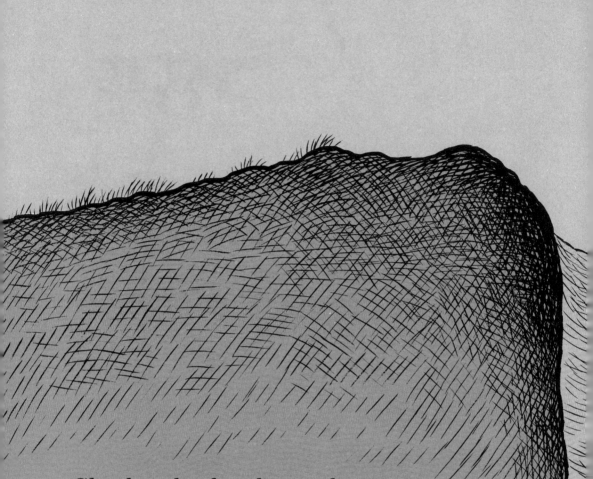

Slowly, slowly, down they came,
Each dog part of a long dog chain.
I reached up. I touched a nose.
I felt them lift me by my toes.
Slowly, slowly, bit by bit,
They dragged me up out of the pit.

I thanked the dogs and Sammy Brown.
And then I started back toward town.
I knew I had to dig once more
To fix things up as they were before.

That's what I did. I dug back gates.

I dug back the garden of Mrs. Thwaites.

I dug back the roosters and the hens.

I dug back all the pigs and their pens.

I dug all day in the summer sun.
I dug back Highway Eighty-One.
I dug back everything in town—
Everything that I'd knocked down.

Today when I dig—well, I'm careful now.
I'm useful too. Sam lets me plow.
He'll never send me to that store
Or tie me up on a hard stone floor.
My dog friends watch and wonder why
They can't dig as well as I.

The Very Bad Bunny

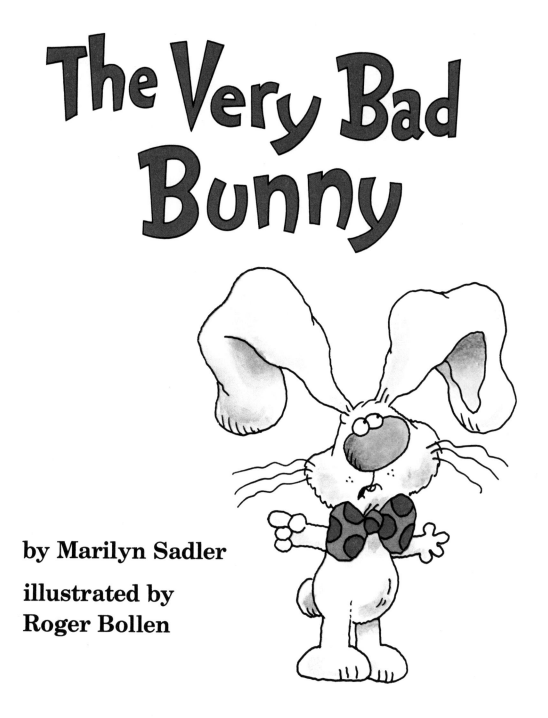

by Marilyn Sadler

illustrated by
Roger Bollen

P. J. Funnybunny did not mean
to be bad.
But sometimes he could not help it.

One morning he spilled
pancake syrup all over
the kitchen floor.

His sister called him a bad bunny.

P. J. said he was sorry.

He did not mean to spill the syrup.

P. J. did not mean to tangle up
his brother's yo-yo either...

or cut up the newspaper
before his father read it . . .

or invite his friends to lunch
without asking his mother.

"I am sorry," said P. J.

But P. J.'s mother sent him

to his room anyway.

That made P. J. so angry,
he threw his pillow out the window.
This time P. J. did mean to be bad!

The Funnybunnys could not believe it.
They had never seen such a bad bunny.

Then one day P. J.'s little cousin
Binky came to visit.

"Now, be good bunnies
and go out and play,"
said P. J.'s mother.
So P. J. and Binky ran out
to play.

But Binky was not a good bunny.

He threw P. J.'s best ball

into the lake.

Then he tossed P. J.'s cowboy hat

into a tree . . .

and broke P. J.'s baseball bat.

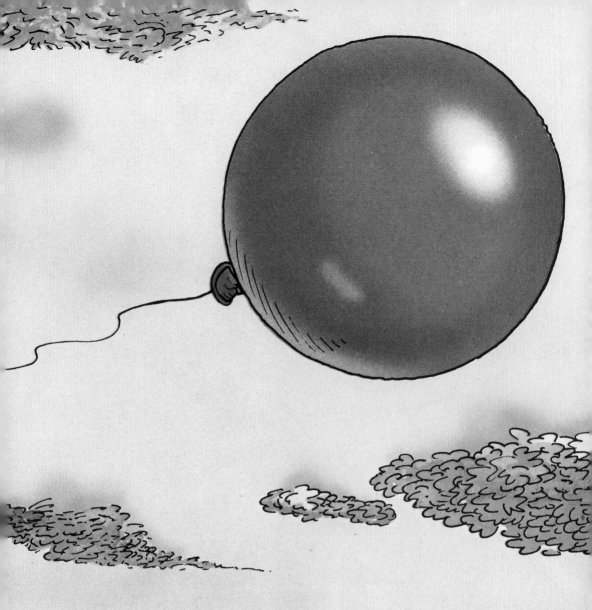

He even let go of P. J.'s balloon.

Binky never once said he was sorry.

"Be nice, Binky!" said P. J.
"Or I will not play with you
anymore."

But Binky did not listen.

He used P. J.'s crayons

without asking . . .

and left them in the sun.

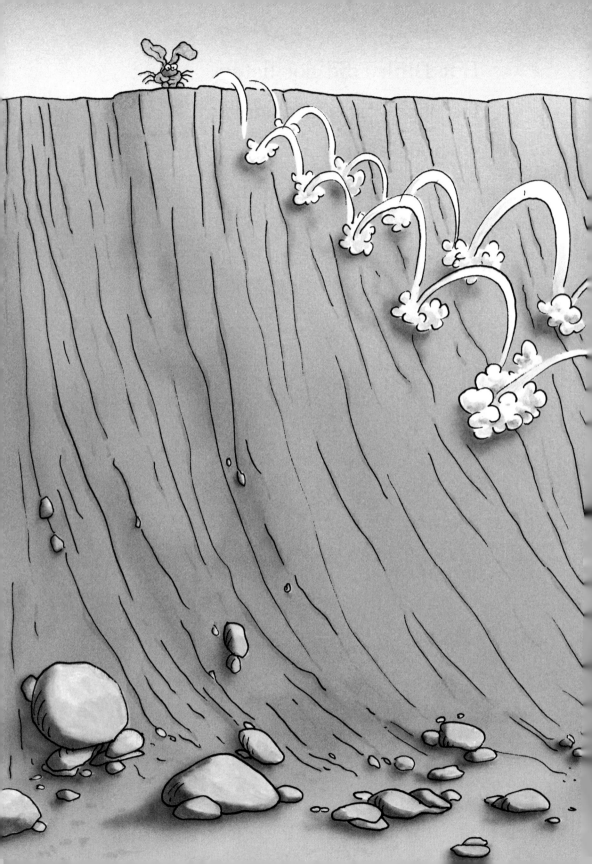

Then he took the wheels off P. J.'s bike.

"THAT does it!" said P. J.

"I'm taking you back to the house!"

But Binky was just as bad
in the house.
First he glued all of P. J.'s
checkers together.

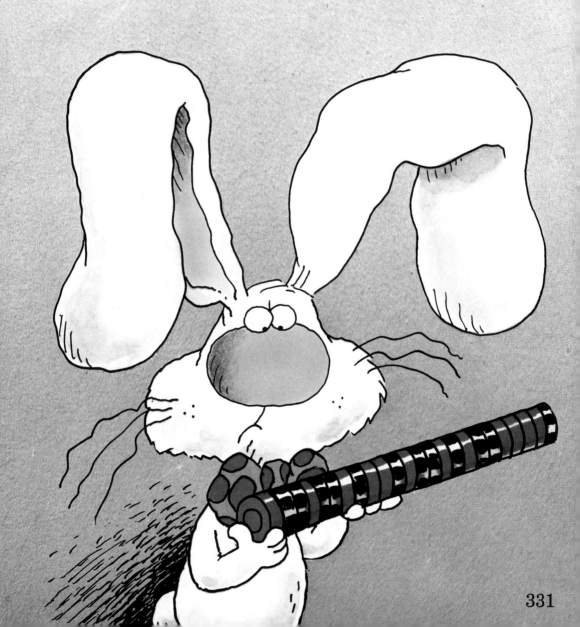

Then he ate the last cookie
in the cookie jar.

He painted bunnies all over
the living room wall.

He put his bubble gum on a chair.

And he locked everyone
out of the house.

338

The Funnybunnys could not
believe it.
They had never seen
such a bad bunny.

Finally it was time
for Binky to go home.
Everyone was so happy
to say good-bye to him.

"Now THAT was a very bad bunny!"
said P. J.

And all the Funnybunnys
had to agree.